Disney's

DOUG ™

Created by
Jim Jinkins

CHRONICLES

Funnie Haunted House

by Tim Grundmann

Illustrated by
Matthew C. Peters, Jeffrey Nodelman, Vinh Truong,
Brian Donnelly, and Miriam Katin

Funnie Haunted House is hand-illustrated by the same
Grade A Quality Jumbo artists who bring you
Disney's Doug, the television series.

JUMBO
PICTURES
GRADE A QUALITY

DISNEP
PRESS
New York

SPECIAL EDITION

Original characters for "The Funnies" developed by Jim Jinkins and
Joe Aaron.

Copyright © 1998 by Disney Enterprises, Inc.

Printed in the United States of America.

1 3 5 7 9 10 8 6 4 2

The artwork for this book is prepared using watercolor.

The text for this book is set in 18-point New Century Schoolbook.

Library of Congress Catalog Card Number: 98-84122

Scholastic Edition
ISBN: 0-7868-4335-7

For more Disney Press fun visit www.DisneyBooks.com.

Funnie Haunted House

pal Skeeter Valentine was shaking him. "Hey, Doug, you okay?"

Doug groaned. "Man," he said, "I sure hate those double-dreams!"

"Wow, Doug," Patti Mayonnaise said. "I never had a Halloween dream before."

They were getting ready to start English class. Doug was still feeling jumpy. "It sure seemed real," he said.

"You should do like I do," Skeeter said. "Take your remote control to bed. So when you have a nightmare, you can change the channel."

"Aaarghhh!" Doug screamed,

and this time it was for real. There was a head right in front of him—a gross, scary head.

Then Doug saw that it was a *fake* head. And holding that head was Roger Klotz!

"Halloween's not for two more days, Roger!" Doug said.

"Just getting a head start, Funnie." Roger laughed. "Get it? A *head* start. Ha-ha-ha!"

Roger howled with laughter. But Doug was steamed. Roger really crossed the line this time. He made him scream in front of Patti!

He was still angry about it later. "That Roger," he said.

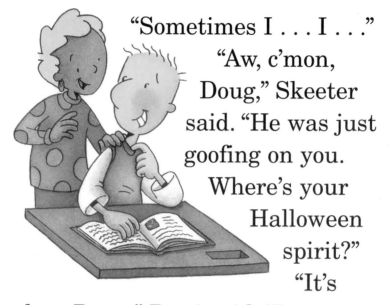

"Sometimes I . . . I . . ." "Aw, c'mon, Doug," Skeeter said. "He was just goofing on you. Where's your Halloween spirit?" "It's okay, Doug," Patti said. "I guess you're just not a Halloween kind of guy. You're more the sweet, sensitive type."

Patti meant it as a compliment, but Doug didn't take it that way. It sounded like he was some kind of cream-puffy, namby-pamby, scaredy-cat chicken!

He remembered how the kids had laughed at Roger's trick. Everyone else thought it was funny. Maybe he *didn't* have the Halloween spirit!

But he would now. He'd be a real Halloween kind of guy! He'd show them!

CHAPTER TWO

Count Funnie
grimly invites you to
a Halloween Costume Party
at Doug's garage of TERROR
on Halloween night!
be there... or Beware!

RIP

Patti giggled. "Doug, your party invitation is great. I can't wait till tomorrow night!"

Doug grinned. All his pals in the school cafeteria were talking about his Halloween party. He couldn't wait, either!

Beebe Bluff sighed. "I can't decide on my costume. Maybe I'll just come as a ghost—a very *rich* ghost."

Then Connie Benge screamed and dropped her glass. *"There's a spider in my water!"*

Doug laughed. "Scared ya!" he

said. "It's just a fake spider in a plastic ice cube!"

Lots of kids in the cafeteria laughed. "Cool trick, Doug!" they shouted. Doug grinned and raised his hands in victory. He *was* a Halloween kind of guy!

"Thanks a lot," Connie groaned. "I spilled water all over my new outfit."

Doug laughed. "Neat trick, huh?"

"Well, at least it's just water, Connie," Patti said gently.

Doug left the cafeteria before the bell rang. He had to get ready for trick number two!

A few minutes before class started,

a messenger came into the class-
room. He was an odd-looking man,
with a big mustache and glasses.
"Telegram for Miss Beebe Bluff,"
he announced in a husky voice.

Beebe beamed. She loved
getting telegrams in class and she
wanted everyone to hear it. "Can
you read it aloud?" she asked.

"Why, of course," the messenger grunted.

"Dear Beebe," he read, "the limo got wrecked and you'll have to walk home from school. Sorry, honey. Love, Daddy."

Beebe's face turned white. "Me . . . ? Walk—home—from—school? No! *No!!*" And she fainted on the spot.

Then the messenger whipped off his mustache and glasses. "Ha! Fooled ya!"

"It's Doug!" the kids laughed. But when Beebe came to, she was furious. "*That's-not-funny!*" she yelled. "How'd you like to be scared like that?"

"Aw, come on, Beebe," Doug

said, "I didn't like it, either, but then I got in the Halloween spirit. Come on, get with it!"

Patti looked at Doug. "Wow, you really did give her a jolt," she said. "Beebe, are you okay?"

"Can you imagine?," Beebe moaned. "*Me* having to walk home from school like a normal,

everyday, common person? It was horrible! Horrible!"

Doug thought Beebe was over-reacting. Maybe *she* should get in the Halloween spirit, he thought.

CHAPTER THREE

"Don't open that locker!" Doug shouted. *"The zombie substitute teacher is in there!"*

On TV, teen star Dillon Farnum opened his school locker. He blinked. He gasped and trembled. Then he screamed in horror at

the gruesome creature inside.
"*Aaaaaaaagh!!!*"

Porkchop covered his eyes.

Doug grinned at him. "C'mon, Porkchop, it's only a movie. Don't be such a scaredy-cat."

Porkchop gave Doug an insulted look.

"Sorry, pal. I mean a scaredy-dog."

Doug taped the rest of *Maniac Zombie Substitute Teacher of Horror High*. He thought he could use some of the scary sound effects for his Garage of Terror.

But then he got an even better idea. Roger's locker door was broken, wasn't it? Doug imagined the

look on his face when he opened
it tomorrow!

The next morning, Roger Klotz
got the shock of his life. He
expected to find his schoolbooks
and smelly old gym shoes inside
his locker. He *didn't* expect to find
snakes inside. Snakes that
jumped out at him!

"*Aaaaaaaagh!!!*" he screamed. He jumped back so far, he fell into his pals Boomer, Willy, and Ned.

Then Doug jumped out from behind a corner. "Scared ya!" he shouted.

Roger looked up and blinked. "Huh?" Then he saw the snakes were the fake kind that spring out of a can. "I mean, I knew they weren't real, Funnie," he said.

"Sure," Doug said. "C'mere, Roger, let me give you a hand."

Roger reached for Doug's hand. But it popped right off his arm! Roger screamed. He threw the hand into the air, then tore down the hallway.

"Way to go, Doug!" a crowd of kids cheered. Doug picked up the hand and took a bow. He was on a roll! He was the King of Halloween!

After school, Doug popped into Swirly's. The place was hopping, as usual. He saw Patti, Skeeter, and Beebe sitting at a table. "Hey, guys," he said. "Ready for my party tonight?"

Beebe gave him a look that could freeze water. *"I'm not speaking to you,"* she said.

Doug grinned. "Aw, c'mon, Beebe. You're not still mad about that fake telegram, are you? I'll make it up to you. Whatever you want—my treat."

"Well, okay," she said. "I'd like a pink convertible with matching leather seats."

"Very funny, Beebe. I mean something *here*," Doug said.

Beebe sighed. "I guess I'll have the Swirly's Halloween Special—pumpkin ice cream with candy corn nuggets."

"Got it," Doug said. He went to the counter and ordered the Halloween Special. When he brought it to the table, he turned around and made a sickening noise.

"Doug!" Patti cried. "What's wrong?"

"Are you all right, Doug?" shouted Skeeter.

Doug turned around and gave Beebe her Swirly's Special—with something extra on top! Everyone gasped.

"Ew! Gross-out!" Beebe cried. She jumped from her seat and rushed off to the girls' room.

"Doug!" Patti shouted. "Are you all right?"

"Ha! Scared ya again!" Doug shouted. "It's just fake puke. See? It's plastic."

All the kids in Swirly's roared with laughter. All except Patti

a bowl of guts on a table. It was just lasagna noodles with red food coloring, but it looked real.

"Are you ready for the party, Frankenchop?"

Porkchop nodded as he hip-hopped to the music. He had bolts in his head and stitches on his face.

"She never leaves a tip
When we go out to eat.
She leaves her eye and a lip
Or her ear and her feet!
Zombie Girlfriend . . . Whoa-oh!"

As Doug sang along, he was unaware that someone was coming up behind him. But when he

 saw the two-headed creature, he jumped about a foot.

"Whoa, sorry, Doug," Skeeter said. "That CD's so loud, you didn't hear me. Didn't mean to scare you."

Doug laughed nervously as he turned down the CD player. "Who, me? Scared? Nah. Cool costume, Skeeter!"

"I just came over to show it to you before the party," he said.

"Guess which head is really mine."

"Er, the one that moves its lips when you talk?" Doug asked.

"Good guess!" Skeeter said.

Doug grinned. "You're just in time for a test run of my Garage of Terror, Skeet." He spoke in a low, creepy voice: "Come this way . . . if you dare. *Ha-ha-ha-ha-ha!*"

Skeeter laughed as Doug led the way through a maze of hanging sheets. "I've prepared some delicious treats for you," he said. "They're on the table to your left. *Ha-ha-ha-ha-ha!*"

Doug shone his flashlight over a bowl of peeled grapes.

"Over here," he said in his creepy voice, "a bowl of scrumptious eyes."

Then a shadow appeared behind a sheet.

"Ah," said Doug, "I see that Frankenchop is hungry again. He's especially fond of eyeballs.

Please, won't you have pity on the poor creature?"

Skeeter giggled and tossed the "eyes" over the sheet. Frankenchop grabbed them and gobbled them up.

Then the lights went out.

"D-D-Doug?" Skeeter stammered.

"Did you turn out the lights?"

"How could I?" Doug asked. "I'm standing right next to you."

Then they heard it. A voice that echoed throughout the garage. A voice right out of a nightmare: *"Get out...GET OUT!!"*

CHAPTER FIVE

"GET...OUT...NOW!!!"

Skeeter whispered, "Uh, Doug, this is just one of your tricks, right?"

Doug whispered back, "N-n-no, Skeeter."

"I-I-I was afraid of that," Skeeter said. Then he shouted. "Doug! Something's got my arm! *Help!*"

"*Help!*" Doug screamed.

"*Help!*" Skeeter shrieked.

Doug flicked on the lights. Porkchop was clinging to Skeeter's arm in fright!

"Boy, were you guys scared!" laughed Doug. "Look, I rigged up this light switch over here. And there's a tape recorder under this table. That's where that scary voice came from. I taped it from *Maniac Zombie Substitute Teacher of Horror High.*"

But Skeeter and Porkchop didn't think it was funny.

"Doug, I asked you if it was a trick, and you said it wasn't. You really spooked me."

"Well, sure, Skeet," Doug said. "If I told you it was a trick, then you wouldn't be scared! C'mon, man, where's your Halloween spirit? Let's finish the tour."

Skeeter hesitated a bit. "Er, sorry, man, I have to, um, go buy some shoes." And he left the garage.

Doug couldn't believe it. "Buy new shoes? Now? What's gotten into him, Porkchop?" he asked.

But Porkchop was gone, too. Then Doug noticed it was getting late. His party was starting in a half-hour!

He rushed up to his room to get ready. He painted his face white,

with fake blood
dripping down
his mouth.
When he
looked in the
mirror, he
almost
scared
himself!
Doug went
downstairs.
He saw Judy in the living room.
She was watching her favorite TV
show, *Shakespeare on Ice*.

Doug crept up behind Judy.
Then he grabbed her shoulders
and screamed, "*Aaarrgghh!*"

Judy shrieked. "*Aaahhhhh!!*"

"Happy Halloween!" Doug
shouted.

Judy trembled in her chair.
"Don't ever . . . *ever* do that
again!"

"Just getting warmed up for my
Halloween party." Doug grinned.

"Let me give you a clue, little

brother," Judy said. "Nobody likes being the butt of somebody else's joke. If I were planning to go to your silly little party—which I am not—I certainly wouldn't go now!"

Doug sighed and went outside to find Porkchop. What did Judy know? She obviously had no Halloween spirit!

Porkchop was sulking inside his tepee. "There you are," Doug said. "Come on, Frankenchop, it's party time!"

Porkchop gave a look that said, "Do you mind?" And he closed the flap of his tepee.

"Not you, too, Porkchop!" Doug

cried. "Come on, it was just a
Halloween trick!"

But it was already eight o'clock.
He had to hurry and greet his
guests.

When Doug got to the garage,
no one was there. He sat down
and waited.

And waited.

He waited a half hour, and still no one came.

Doug wondered if maybe he had given everyone the wrong time for the party. He went into the kitchen and phoned Skeeter's house, but there was no answer.

Then he called Beebe's house. The Bluff's butler answered the phone. "Miss Beebe cannot come to the telephone," he said in a snotty voice. "She's having a Halloween party." And he hung up.

Doug's mom and dad came into the kitchen. "How's the party going, Douglas?" his mother asked.

Doug hung up the phone slowly. "They didn't come," he said in a quiet voice. "They're having their own party at Beebe's."

CHAPTER SIX

Doug's parents looked at each other a moment. Then Mrs. Funnie said quietly, "I'm sorry, honey."

"Aw, man!" Doug said. "I've been working on my Garage of Terror for two whole days!" Then he thought a minute and said, "I guess Judy was right."

"What do you mean, Douglas?" his mother asked.

"Well," Doug said sadly. "I guess I've been playing Halloween tricks on my friends and making them the butt of my jokes." And he told his parents about the spider in Connie's glass, and the fake telegram to Beebe. He also told them about his fake vomit trick at Swirly's and how he had scared Skeeter in the Garage of Terror.

Mr. Funnie sighed. "Doug, no one likes being ridiculed. Getting laughs at someone else's expense is never funny."

"It was all just pretend!" Doug protested.

"But they didn't know that, dear," Mrs. Funnie said. "Do you see the difference?"

Doug nodded slowly. His mother hugged him and asked him if he wanted some hot chocolate. "No, thanks," he said. "I think I'll start cleaning up the party stuff."

Doug went out to the garage and sat down. He wanted to be alone. He remembered the look on Connie's face

when she saw the spider in her water. And how Beebe fainted when she got the fake telegram.

He remembered how scared he was when Roger dangled that fake head in front of him and how mad he had gotten when Roger had made him scream. And *he* had scared his pals just as much! He didn't realize it at the time, because he was trying so hard to be cool and not some sweet, sensitive guy! Now he felt awful.

The lights went out.

Doug sat in the darkness. His heart started pounding. *Okay, keep calm*, he told himself. It was probably just the fuse. He'd just

walk over to the fuse box and—

Doug froze. He heard voices. Whispering voices. So quiet at first, he thought he was imagining it. But then the voices got louder: *"Are you scared? Are you scared?"*

He must be imagining it! But the darkness made everything creepy. The only light in the garage was the dim glow from the jack-o'-lantern.

It began to move. *"Heh-heh-heh,"* it said.

Then the glow-in-the-dark skeleton started bobbing up and down. *"Hee-hee-hee!"* it said.

Doug felt the little hairs on the back of his neck stick up. Then he remembered there was a flashlight on his dad's workbench. He inched his way in the dark toward it. He groped on the table for the flashlight. Then something grabbed his leg!

"*He-e-e-lp!*" he shouted.

Doug yelled like crazy. He found the flashlight and switched it on. And what he saw chilled his bones.

Creatures. Horrible, monstrous creatures in the Garage of Terror! A werewolf girl. A zombie. A ghost. A horrible ghoul covered in seaweed. And a mummy was holding on to Doug's leg!

Creatures that laughed from the shadows. Creatures that shuffled toward him, their arms stretched out. *"Are you scared?"* they asked over and over. *"Are you scared, Doug?"*

For the first time that Halloween, Doug was really and truly scared. He thought the creatures were after him for scaring everyone!

"Yes!" Doug cried. "I'm scared! And I promise I'll never scare anyone again!"

CHAPTER SEVEN

"Do you mean it, Doug?" the werewolf girl asked.

The lights flicked on. Doug blinked in amazement at the werewolf in a cheerleader outfit. "Connie!" he shouted.

Then the ghoul covered in seaweed said, "I guess it worked, guys!"

"Patti!" Doug cried.

He could now see the "creatures" clearly. Beebe was costumed as a rich ghost, dripping with jewelry. Skunky Beaumont came as a surfer-zombie. Chalky Studebaker came as a Martian football player, and the Sleech brothers came as themselves— only carrying their own heads!

Then the mummy laughed. "Payback time, Funnie!"

"Roger!" Doug said. The little mummy next to him was Roger's cat, Stinky. She didn't look too happy about being covered in toilet paper. "But how—?"

"We snuck in here when you

went inside," the two-headed
Skeeter said. "We spooked ya,
huh, Doug?"

Doug sat down and sighed.
"Man, did you ever. I thought you
guys weren't coming!"

"We wouldn't do that to you,
Doug," Patti said. "But this was

the only way you'd understand what you put us through."

Doug nodded. "I guess I went overboard, huh? If I made you guys feel the way I just felt now, then I'm really, really sorry."

"Ah, what's the big deal?" complained Roger. "It was just a few little Halloween tricks."

"That's okay, Doug," Patti said gently, ignoring Roger. "Sometimes it's fun to be scared—when you're with your friends and you know it's just pretend. But when you make people think it actually *is* real and it makes fun of someone else, then it's not fun anymore."

Doug nodded. "Like my fake puke trick at Swirly's?"

"You owe me *eighteen* Swirly Specials for that one, Doug," Beebe said.

Porkchop poked his head into the garage. Doug sighed. "I'm sorry, pal," he said. "Can you forgive me, too?"

Porkchop seemed to consider it for a moment. Then he wagged his tail.

"Hey, what is this," Roger said, "a Halloween party or the Boo-Hoo-I'm-Sorry party?"

Patti gave Doug a friendly punch on his arm. "C'mon, Doug," she said, "let's get this party rolling. I bet I can beat your bobbing-for-beets record."

Doug's face broke into a smile. "No way!" he said. "I'll beat my own beet-bobbing record!"

And he ran to the beet-bobbing bucket to prove it.

Dear Journal:

Well, Halloween's over, and it was one I'll never forget. I guess practical jokes aren't all that practical after all. I'll sure think twice before giving someone a good scare again!

Like Porkchop. He's watching *Revenge of Maniac Zombie Substitute Teacher of Horror High* on his little TV right now. You should see the look on his face! I wonder what he'd do if I snuck up on him real quiet and went—

Boo!

But I won't!

WHOOPS!

Doug was about to take the attendance list to the school office. But he tripped in a trash can. Now all of the names are mixed up. He can't turn them over to Vice Principal Bone like that! Can you help Doug unscramble the names of all the kids in his class?

1. UDGO
2. TIATP
3. EGORR
4. KETRESE
5. YLAKHC
6. OMOBER
7. EDN
8. LYILW
9. NIENCO
10. NKUKSY
11. CKTUNREF
12. EBEEB

1. Doug   2. Patti   3. Roger   4. Skeeter
5. Chalky   6. Boomer   7. Ned   8. Willy
9. Connie   10. Skunky   11. Fentruck   12. Beebe

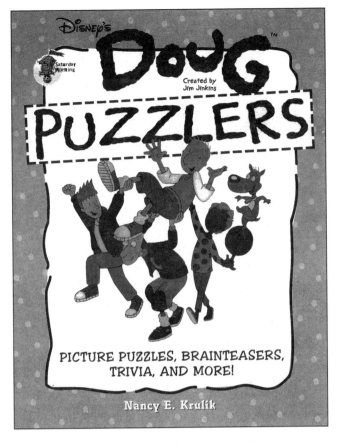

Your Favorite

Disney Characters

Disney's BEAUTY AND THE BEAST
Belle's Story
$3.95 each ($5.50 CAN)

PEPPER ANN:
Soccer Sensation
$3.95 each ($5.50 CAN)

RECESS:
The Experiment
$3.95 each ($5.50 CAN)

RECESS:
The New Kid
$3.95 each ($5.50 CAN)

Disney's Cinderella
$3.95 each ($5.50 CAN)

Your Favorite

Disney Books

Disney's HERCULES
I Made Herc
a Hero: By Phil
$3.50 each ($4.95 CAN)

Disney's ALADDIN
Jasmine's Story
$3.50 each ($4.95 CAN)

Disney's TOY STORY
I Come in Peace
$3.50 each ($4.95 CAN)

Disney's 101 DALMATIANS
Cruella Returns
$3.50 each ($4.95 CAN)

Disney's
THE LITTLE MERMAID
Flounder to the Rescu
$3.50 each ($4.95 CAN)

Read all the

Disney Chapters

Disney's FLUBBER
My Story
$3.50 each ($4.95 CAN)

Doug's
Big Comeback
$3.50 each ($4.95 CAN)

Doug's
Hoop Nightmare
$3.50 each ($4.95 CAN)

Doug's
Vampire Caper
$3.50 each ($4.95 CAN)

Disney's THE LION KING:
Just Can't Wait
To Be King
$3.50 each ($4.95 CAN)